The Bubblegum Tree

The Bubblegum Tree

Alexander McCall Smith

illustrations by Ian Bilbey

BLOOMSBURY

This is for George Stevenson

This edition published in Great Britain in 2005 by Bloomsbury Publishing Plc,
36 Soho Square, London, W1D 3QY

First published in the UK by Scholastic Ltd, 1996

Text copyright © 1996 by Alexander McCall Smith
Illustrations copyright © 2005 by Ian Bilbey
The moral rights of the author and illustrator have been asserted

A CIP record of this book is available from the
British Library

ISBN 0 7475 8053 7
Printed in Great Britain by Clays Ltd, St Ives plc

10 9 8 7 6 5 4 3 2 1

All papers u   oducts

The

CHAPTER 1

In the Bubblegum Works

Have you ever visited a bubblegum factory? No? Neither had Billy, even though there was one right on the edge of his town. There it stood – the Better Bubblegum Works – with its tall chimney and its two very grand gates, both painted bubblegum pink.

This factory was run by a man called Mr Walter Alliwallah Pravindar Gopal, usually just called Mr Gopal, or even Walter. Mr Gopal was a well-known man in the town, and very popular with everybody. As he walked down the street, people would say, 'Good morning, Mr Gopal. Fine day, isn't it?'

Mr Gopal would beam at them in a very friendly manner and say, 'Excellent day! Oh, yes it is! Very fine indeed!' And as often as not, he would reach into his pocket and offer them a stick of Gopal's Best Pink Bubblegum, wonderfully fresh from the factory. People like this.

Billy and his sister, Nicola, always greeted Mr Gopal very politely, and were usually rewarded with a stick or two of bubblegum. They thought Mr Gopal was quite the friend-liest person they had ever met and were both very proud that he had chosen their town in which to build his famous factory.

Then, one day, Billy saw Mr Gopal walking down the street, shaking his head and looking rather sad.

'Good morning, Mr Gopal,' said Billy. 'It's a nice day, isn't it?'

Mr Gopal looked at Billy sadly.

'I am sorry to say, Billy,' he began, 'that

7

even if it's a nice day, I'm not enjoying it at all. Dear me!'

Billy was astonished. Nobody had ever known Mr Gopal to look sad. There must be something very seriously the matter.

'Is there something wrong at the factory?' he asked.

'Yes,' said Mr Gopal, shaking his head again. 'There is something very wrong at the factory, and if you come along with me I shall show you exactly what it is.'

Billy was excited to be going into the bubblegum factory, even if Mr Gopal seemed in such a sad mood. As he accompanied Mr Gopal in the front door, he smelled the wonderful smell of bubblegum – a smell like no other smell. It was a *pink* sort of smell – a smell that seemed to get bigger as you smelled at it and then burst, just like the popping of a bubble.

'This way,' said Mr Gopal. 'We shall go to my office.'

Billy followed Mr Gopal past the great bubblegum-making machines, all humming and whirring away in a most energetic fashion. It was all very interesting to see, but Billy was worried and could not enjoy himself as much as he would have liked.

Mr Gopal showed Billy into his office and sat him down on a chair.

'Here,' he said, taking a piece of bubblegum from a tray on his desk. 'This is a piece of bubblegum, is it not?'

'Yes,' said Billy, looking at the stick of Gopal's Best.

'I'd like you to unwrap it,' said Mr Gopal, passing the stick to Billy. 'Then pop it in your mouth and chew hard.'

Billy was rather puzzled, but did as he was told. He slipped the pink stick out of its silver paper and put it into his mouth. Then he began to chew. It tasted fine, and the smell – well, that was exactly the same as it always was.

'Now,' said Mr Gopal. 'I'd like you to

blow a bubble. Just an ordinary bubble.'

Billy moved the gum around his mouth, getting it to just the right place for blowing a bubble. Then he blew.

He blew hard. Then he blew again. A moment or two later a small bit of gum popped out of his mouth, and a tiny, almost invisible bubble appeared. Then it burst – with a little pop, like a frog's hiccup – and was gone.

Billy sucked the gum back in. 'I'll try again,' he said. 'That wasn't very good.'

'Oh dear,' said Mr Gopal, ringing his hands. 'It won't make any difference. You can try and try again, it'll all be the same. You won't do any better than that.'

Mr Gopal was right. Try as he might, Billy could not blow a proper bubble. There was something very badly wrong with the gum.

'It's hopeless,' said Mr Gopal. 'The gum just isn't the same as it used to be.'

'But what's gone wrong?' asked Billy, dropping the useless bubblegum into the bin. 'Why won't it work?'

'It's a very strange story,' said Mr Gopal. 'Would you like me to tell you all about it?'

'Yes,' said Billy, feeling very sorry for the dejected bubblegum manufacturer. 'Maybe I can help.'

So Mr Gopal told Billy about what had happened. And it was indeed a very strange tale – stranger than anything Billy had heard before.

CHAPTER 2

A Very Strange Story

'I got my recipe for bubblegum from my father,' began Mr Gopal. 'He was a very famous bubblegum manufacturer in his time – even more famous than I am. He lived in India, in a town called Bombay, which is a marvellous, exciting place, I can tell you.

'He had a big bubblegum factory where he used to make a bubblegum called Bombay

Best Bubbly. His business was a great success, but I'm sorry to say that one day a terrible fire burned the whole factory down – right to the ground. Nobody knew how it started, but it destroyed all my father's property and he lost just about everything he had in this life. It even burned off my father's moustache. It had been a wonderful moustache; now it was just a tiny, scorched line.

'So from being a rich man, my father became a poor man. Fortunately, there were one or two possessions which he kept away from the factory, at home. These included an old black money box with two thousand rupees in it, and a small black book which he always hid under his pillow. That was about all.

'I remember the day after the fire, when my father came back to the house and called me into the front room. He stood there, with his sad moustache, and his eyes all watering from the smoke.

'"I am an old man," he said, "and I want

to say something very important to you. You are my only child, Walter Alliwallah Pravindar Gopal, and you are all I am going to leave behind in the world. So I just want to say this to you. Remember that a Gopal is always a brave man – always – and there is nothing he is scared to do. Your grandfather, Sikrit Pal Praviwallah Gopal, was not even frightened of tigers and fought one with his bare hands when it attacked him. He bit its tail so hard that the tiger jumped off his back and retreated into the jungle. That isn't at all unusual for a Gopal. That is how a Gopal behaves.

'"The second thing I want to say to you is this. Now that I am a poor man, I cannot leave you great riches on this earth. All I have is this box of a few rupees and this book. Use the rupees to go off and make your fortune, and use what is in the book to start a great bubblegum factory again. Remember that the Gopals have always been bubblegum people."

'And with that my father gave me the box and the book. Then he reached out and touched me lightly on the head, went into his room, and put on a simple white robe. After

that, he said goodbye to me, shook my hand, and walked out of the house.

'I watched him walk down the path from the house and then off on to the dusty road. People do that in India. When they reach a certain time of life, they sometimes just walk off and become holy men and never come back. That is what my father did.

'My eyes were filled with tears as I watched him go. I knew, though, that this was what he wanted to do – his heart, you see, was broken when his factory burned down. Then, a short while later I set off on my own travels. These eventually brought me here – to this town – where I worked hard, day and night, until I had saved enough money to build the bubblegum factory in which you are sitting right at this very moment.'

Mr Gopal was silent for a moment, and Billy wondered whether he had come to the end of his story. But he had not.

'You will be asking yourself, Billy, *What*

was in that book? Well, I shall tell you.

'When I opened the book, I had a great surprise. I don't know quite what I had expected to find inside, but all that I saw was line after line of writing *that made no sense at all.* My father, you must realise, had written the whole thing in code, and he had forgotten to give me the key!

'So I sat and looked at the meaningless jumble of letters and tried to make some sense of it. What on earth could *momixaying bomowl* mean? And why did the word *gomum* keep appearing? I was quite at a loss as to what to do, and so I just carried the little book around with me, tucked away in my inside pocket.

'Then a short while later, on a long train journey from Bombay, I found myself sitting opposite a man who was busy doing a cross-word puzzle. It was a hot afternoon, and I was half asleep as the train chugged along on its journey. But then, as my eyes rested on my fellow passenger, I was brought back to wakefulness by the sheer speed with which he was solving the clues. His pencil seemed to dart across the paper like a bird, filling in the letters, and in no time at all he had finished the puzzle.

'I sat bolt upright.

'"Excuse me, sir," I said. "I noticed that you were very quick in solving that puzzle. I wonder if you could help me."

'The other man looked at me over the glasses that were perched on the tip of his nose.

'"You are addressing Mr PJ Lal," he said, "the crossword puzzle champion of all India. If it is a crossword clue that is worrying you, then you are undoubtedly speaking to the right man."

'I was encouraged by his helpfulness, and I immediately took out my little book and opened it before him.

'"This was given to me by my father," I said. "And he did not give me the key to his code. It contains something I am very keen to read."

'Mr PJ Lal took the book from me and examined the writing.

'"May I ask you what your father's name was?" he said.

'I told him, and he wrote the letters of his name out on a strip of paper. Then the stub of pencil darted about, scribbling other letters underneath and moving them about. I watched in fascination and was very disappointed when, after several minutes, Mr PJ Lal shook his head.

'"And what was the name of your grandfather?" he asked.

'I told him, and on another strip of paper he wrote out, in large letters: SIKRIT PAL PRAVIWALLAH GOPAL. Again there was much scribbling as he juggled with letters. Then he shook his head once more.

'"May I ask where your father was born?" he said.

'"Bombay, of course," I replied.

'Mr PJ Lal looked thoughtful for a few moments, but then he burst out laughing.

'"Very simple," he said. "Take the Bs out of Bombay and you get OM and AY, do you not?"

'He did not wait for me to answer.

'"Put an OM before each vowel – that is before any A, E, I, O or U. Then put an AY before the next vowel, and there you are."

'I was not sure what he meant, and so he leaned forward and showed me.

'"Bubblegum becomes BOMUBBLAYE-GOMUM," he explained. "And these words MOMIXAYING BOMOWL are simply mixing bowl. Do you see what I mean?"

'I had to agree. It was quite simple, and now, with a little effort, I could read what my father had written.

'I looked up to thank Mr PJ Lal, but he was already on his feet, reaching for his suit-case, as we were arriving at a station. He smiled at me, put his hat on his head, and disappeared, and I am always sorry that I could not have rewarded him in some way for what he did. But I had the key to the code now, and for the rest of the journey I sat and read the very strange story which my father had written down.'

CHAPTER 3

The Story of the Bubblegummies

'Was it a recipe?' asked Billy.

'Yes,' said Mr Gopal. 'There *was* a recipe. But there was much more besides. My father, you see, not only told me what to put in the bubblegum, but where to get it.'

Billy was puzzled. 'Can't you just buy the ingredients from a supermarket – like anything else?'

'Oh, you can do that if you want to make just any old bubblegum,' said Mr Gopal. 'But if you want to make real bubblegum, bubblegum that remains wonderfully chewy for days and days, you have to put something very special in it.'

Mr Gopal paused. 'Can you keep a secret, Billy?'

Billy nodded. He had always been good at keeping secrets, even those that were really very difficult to keep.

'In that case,' said Mr Gopal, 'I shall tell you what was in that book.

'My father told me that right back in the days when he started his factory, one of the men who worked there came to his office. This man, who came from a remote part of India – a place where there are still great jungles and empty hills – told my father that he had something which would make his bubblegum even better. So my father asked him to show it to him.

'The man took a square of a rubbery pink

substance out of his pocket. He handed this to my father and said, "This is from the bubblegum tree which grows in our jungle at home. If you add it to your bubblegum, it will make it the finest in the world."

'Of course, my father did not believe him at first, but when he examined the curious, rubbery square, it smelled so good that he decided to try it. And it worked, just as the man said it would. It made the bubblegum wonderfully soft and chewy. So there must be a bubblegum tree after all!

'Well, my father was thrilled. And he was even more thrilled when the man told him that the people he knew up in the jungle would send a regular supply of this new raw gum, which they did. And in return, every month, my father sent money to repay them for their trouble. These people, he said, were called the Bubblegummies, and they seemed very friendly and gentle people indeed.

'My father wrote in his book exactly how to

get in touch with the Bubblegummies – he even drew a map – and he also explained just how much gum should go into the mixture. And so, when I opened my own bubblegum factory, I wrote to these people, and received a very friendly letter back from them.

'They said that they were very sorry to hear about my father's fire, and that they would be quite happy to send me squares of raw gum whenever I needed them.

'And that's why my bubblegum has always been so chewy – and tasted so good as well. Every month without fail, a parcel has arrived from India with supplies of the gum. Then, two months ago, the parcel failed to turn up, and since then I have heard nothing from the Bubblegummies – nothing at all. I wrote to them, of course, but the post office from which they used to collect their mail sent my letter back to me. Nobody had collected it, they said.

'And that, Billy, is why you see me looking

so sad. I am very worried that something has happened to the Bubblegummies.'

After Mr Gopal had told this story, they both sat silently for a little while. Then at last Billy spoke.

'Why don't you go and find out what's happened?' he asked. 'Maybe there's a very simple explanation.'

Mr Gopal looked at him in astonishment. 'Do you mean – go to the jungle?'

Billy nodded. 'Yes,' he said. 'Surely somebody would be able to take you there.'

Mr Gopal stared at Billy. 'But I couldn't possibly do that,' he protested. 'Oh no. I couldn't possibly go off to the jungle all by myself. There are ... well, there are *tigers* and things like that out there.' As he spoke, he gave a slight shudder.

Billy thought for a moment. 'You could go with somebody,' he said. 'You needn't go alone.'

'But I don't know anybody who would want

to go to the jungle,' wailed Mr Gopal. Then he paused, looking hard at Billy. 'You wouldn't help me, would you, Billy? You wouldn't come to the jungle with me?'

Billy gave his answer immediately. 'Of course I'd come. And my sister Nicola would come too. We'd both come with you.'

Mr Gopal heaved a sigh of relief. 'Well, in that case, I shall be happy to go. We should make plans immediately.'

'There's one problem,' said Billy. 'India's a very long way away. How shall we get there?'

Mr Gopal only had to think for a moment. 'That will be quite simple,' he said. 'I have an aunt who has a flying boat.'

'A flying boat?' asked Billy.

'Yes,' said Mr Gopal. 'It's a very old aeroplane that used to fly all the way out to India, landing on lakes and the sea on the way. It's a funny old plane, but I'm sure that Aunty would be quite delighted to have an excuse to get it going again.'

Then Mr Gopal stopped, as if he had suddenly found a flaw in their plan.

'Will your parents let you go?' he asked doubtfully. 'Some parents would get very worried about their children going off to India in flying boats. You know how parents are. Do you think yours are like that?'

'Not at all,' said Billy. 'I'm sure that they'll say yes – if you agree to bring us back safely.'

Mr Gopal nodded. 'It will be a great adventure,' he said. 'But I'm sure that it's the sort of adventure that one comes back from safe and sound. So why not go and ask them right now? Then we can get everything ready.'

Billy was right.

'Off to India?' said his father, when he told him of Mr Gopal's invitation. 'In a flying boat? Sounds like a splendid idea to me! I wish I could come too, but I'm just too busy at the moment.'

And the children's mother said much the same thing.

'The jungle!' she exclaimed. 'What a wonderful adventure! Of course you can go. But promise me you'll be extremely careful of snakes and tigers, and things like that.'

CHAPTER 4

Off to India!

It was a wonderful trip. With Mr Gopal reading the maps, and his aunt at the controls, the faithful old plane droned its way across mountains, plains, and long stretches of sea. Nicola and Billy passed sandwiches around and poured tea for everybody from large flasks which they had brought with them. And from time to time they slept, although it was generally far too exciting to do much of that.

They had to stop every now and then to fill the tanks of the plane and to allow Mr Gopal's aunt to have a rest. They landed in Egypt, on the river Nile, and watched the white-sailed boats drift by. Then they landed on the sea beside a desert, and watched the camels plod their way over the sand dunes at the water's edge. And finally, after several days of travel, Mr Gopal looked up from his map and announced that unless he was mistaken – which of course he wasn't – the smudge of land down below them was the coast of India.

They still had some way to go, as the jungle they were looking for was quite a distance from the coast. But Mr Gopal's map was very accurate, and he guided his aunt right to the very river where they could land the flying boat. She landed the plane perfectly, hardly making a ripple on the water, and there they were, on the river at the edge of the jungle.

The engines of the plane stopped and the propellers came to a halt. It was terribly quiet now, after the roar of the engines had died away, and the jungle seemed very thick.

'Are you sure we're in the right place?' asked Billy. 'It all seems very deserted to me.'

'One hundred per cent sure,' said Mr Gopal. 'Or almost . . .'

They stared out of the window of the plane. The edge of the river was lined with great trees, which seemed to get even taller further away. It looked as if it would be very difficult to go anywhere in jungle as thick as that. But then Mr Gopal gave a cry.

'There it is!' he said. 'Over there. A clearing – in just the place the map said it would be!'

They tied the plane to a tree at the water's edge. Then, carefully looking where they were putting their feet, they stepped out of the plane and into the grassy clearing.

'I think we should sit down and have a cup

of tea,' said Mr Gopal's aunt, producing a flask. 'It's been a very long flight.'

The children were keen to start exploring, but they knew that there would be plenty of time for that. So they all sat down and sipped at their tea while they looked at the jungle around them. From close up, it seemed even thicker than it had looked from the window of the plane, and they wondered how they could possibly find anybody in all that greenery.

Suddenly Billy reached out and tapped Nicola on the arm.

'Don't stare too hard,' he whispered, 'but I'm quite sure that that bush over there moved!'

Nicola followed his gaze to a large bush at the edge of the clearing.

'You must be imagining things,' she whispered back. 'It's just a bush.'

And at that moment, the bush moved again. It did not move far, but it moved, and both children gave a start.

'Mr Gopal,' whispered Billy. 'There's a moving bush –'

He did not have time to finish. The bush now dashed across the clearing, making for the far side.

'Mr Gopal!' shouted Billy. 'Look at that bush!'

As he called out, Billy leapt up and stuck out his leg, right in the way of the moving bush. There was a grunt, followed by a muffled cry, and over went the bush in a shower of leaves. Then, from the middle of the fallen bush, there emerged a rather tall man.

He looked at Billy.

'You really should be more careful,' he said. 'I could have taken a painful fall.'

'I'm sorry,' said Billy. 'I thought you were just a bush. I didn't know . . .'

The man turned away, looking rather annoyed, and spoke to Mr Gopal.

'And who may you be?' he asked directly.

'I am Walter Alliwallah Pravindar Gopal,' said Mr Gopal.

The man seemed very surprised. 'Oh!' he exclaimed. 'Do you mean you are *the* Walter Alliwallah Pravindar Gopal?'

'I believe so,' said Mr Gopal.

The man broke into a smile. 'In that case, I needn't even have bothered to spy on you at all! So you are Walter Alliwallah Pravindar Gopal! Well, well, well!'

'Are you one of the Bubblegummies?' asked Mr Gopal.

The man nodded enthusiastically and began to shake hands with everybody.

'I am Mr Bhalla,' he said. 'And you are all very welcome. I'm sorry that I seemed so suspicious to begin with. Please, come with me. I can't say we were expecting you, but everybody will be very pleased that you have arrived.'

They followed the man along a path through the jungle. Billy had never been in a jungle before, and found it very strange and delicious to be walking through the green light that filtered down from above. He noticed the trailing vines, and the orchids, and the broad-leaved ferns. He noticed the butterflies – bigger than any he had ever seen before – and the twisted roots of the great trees. It was an intriguing, wonderful place.

'Almost there,' called out Mr Bhalla after a while. 'Just a little way to go.'

The jungle had now thinned out, and they seemed to be reaching the edge of a plain, with dotted trees, and mountains in the distance.

'We don't actually live in the jungle itself,' said Mr Bhalla. 'We prefer to be just on the edge. And now, if you look closely, you'll see our place up ahead.'

They all looked ahead. There was a lot of grass, and a large cluster of tall trees, but nothing else.

'I can't see any houses,' said Mr Gopal's aunt. 'Are you sure we've come the right way?'

'Ah,' said Mr Bhalla, smiling broadly. 'Perhaps you should look up a bit rather than down.'

They looked up, and it was Nicola who saw it first.

'Look,' she cried, pointing at the trees. 'There's a house!'

'That's right,' said Mr Bhalla. 'That's my brother's house, actually. Mine is a bit further on, in that large tree with the bushy top. And over there, at the far end, is the school. And the hospital is over there. It has two trees all to itself.'

Billy was astonished, and as they drew closer to the trees, his astonishment grew. The Bubblegummies had made an entire village in the trees! Craning his neck, Billy could see just how skilfully they had made it. Each house, which was beautifully fashioned out of wood, was connected to the tree next to it by a wooden walkway, and that tree would be connected to the tree beyond, and so on. There were ladders, too, which led from level to level, and swinging bridges, knotted with vines, crossing the wider spaces. You could live entirely in the trees, it seemed.

Mr Bhalla led them to the bottom of a

large tree, looked up into the branches, and whistled. For a moment nothing happened, and he whistled again. Then, out of the thick leaves above, there appeared a long ladder, being lowered slowly down to them.

'Please,' he said, gesturing politely. 'Please climb up here.'

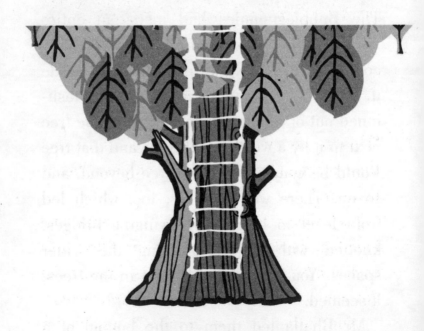

CHAPTER 5

Gumgee Jumping

'This is my house,' said Mr Bhalla, when they reached the top of the ladder. 'Please come in.'

They followed him into the tree house, and found themselves in a large room filled with colourful furniture. Mr Bhalla asked them to sit down, and then went off to fetch refreshments.

'Now, what is the trouble?' asked Mr

41

Gopal, as they sipped at long glasses of a delicious pink sherbet drink which Mr Bhalla had given them.

Mr Bhalla put down his glass. 'If you come to this window, you'll see,' he said.

They crossed the room, which was swaying gently as the tree moved with the breeze. Mr Bhalla opened a window and pointed to the edge of the jungle.

'Our bubblegum trees grow on the edge of the jungle,' he said. 'They're very old trees. Each tree has to grow for at least a hundred years before it gives up any gum. Fortunately, nobody ever thought of cutting them down before, and so we've had a good number of trees. But now . . .'

Billy looked out of the window towards the jungle. Was that a plume of smoke in the distance? Or was it a cloud?

'Do you mean somebody is cutting them down?' asked Mr Gopal, sounding shocked.

'Yes,' said Mr Bhalla. 'They are. It started a few months ago. Some men came and set up camp further up the river. Then they started to cut down our trees. They have wonderful wood, you see – there's nothing else quite like it. They cut down our trees and float them down the river to a sawmill.'

Billy was outraged. 'But they're *your* trees!' he exclaimed. 'You've always looked after them!'

Mr Bhalla sighed. '*We* think they're our trees, but these men say otherwise. We've tried to stop them, but they've just run after us with their axes and chased us away. There's nothing we can do. Maybe it would be different if we were different people, but Bubblegummies don't like fighting – we never have.'

Mr Bhalla returned to his chair and sank his head in his hands.

'So that's why you haven't been getting your gum,' he said. 'And if things go on as they are, in a few months they will have cut all the trees down and that will be the end of the bubblegum tree – for ever.'

Nobody said anything. Billy thought that he had never heard such a sad story before. Surely somebody could think of something? Surely somebody could do something to save the bubblegum trees before it was too late.

Mr Bhalla invited them all to stay, and showed them to their rooms in his tree house. Then, since they had a few hours before dinner, Billy and Nicola set off to explore the Bubblegummie village.

It was a marvellous, exciting place. Everybody was very friendly, and when they met some children coming out of the school, their new friends quickly agreed to show them round. They took them along all the walkways and swinging bridges, and even showed them up the lookout ladders that led to the very tops of the trees.

'Why do you live in tree houses?' asked Billy.

'Why not?' said one of the Bubblegummie

boys. 'Wouldn't you prefer to live in a tree house?'

'I suppose I would,' said Billy. 'You get a much better view. And it's cooler. And your house would never get flooded in the rain.'

'That's it,' said the boy. 'That's why we live up here.'

Most exciting of all, though, was the emergency exit. This was right in the middle of the village, at the top of one of the tallest trees, and it was shown to Billy and Nicola by the Bubblegummie boy.

'We have to have a way of getting down to the ground in a hurry,' he said. 'Like if somebody fell, or if there were a fire. This is what we do.'

He showed them to a platform to which a thick pink rope was tied.

'You hold the end of this rope,' he said, 'and then you jump.'

Billy inspected the rope. It had a very strange feel to it.

'This feels like bubblegum,' he said.

'And that's just what it is,' said the boy. 'We use bubblegum for all sorts of things.'

He took the end of the rope from Billy's hand. 'Let me show you,' he said. 'Please stand back.'

Billy and Nicola watched as the boy tucked the end of the rope into his belt. Then, without any further warning, he leapt over the edge of the platform.

The two children gave a gasp as they saw the boy plummet down.

'He's going to hit the ground!' screamed Nicola. 'Oh, look out!'

But Nicola was wrong. The long bubble-gum rope played out swiftly, but then stopped, and began to stretch. It was just like a great piece of elastic, and it brought the boy to a stop just before he hit the ground. Then, with a loud twanging noise, the rope jerked him back up, shooting through the air, to land on his feet on the platform.

'There you are,' said the boy. 'It's quite

simple. If I had wanted to get off at the bottom, I would just have slipped the rope out of my belt. But it's just as easy to come back up again.'

Billy laughed. 'It's just like bungee jumping,' he exclaimed.

'Gumgee jumping,' the boy corrected him. 'We invented it you see. The Bubble-gummies were the first to do it – not that anybody knows about that!'

He passed the end of the rope to Billy.

'Would you like to try?' he asked. 'It's very simple.'

Billy's heart gave a leap. The ground was a very long way away. What if the bubblegum rope broke?

'I'm not sure,' he stammered. 'Maybe tomorrow . . .'

'I'll go,' said Nicola, reaching for the rope. 'It looks like great fun.'

Billy held his breath as Nicola launched herself into space. He would get into terrible trouble, he thought, if the rope broke, and he had to take Nicola home all covered in plaster. But it did not, and within seconds his sister was back up on the platform, beaming with pleasure. After that, Billy had to do it himself, and he found it just as easy as the boy had said. So they each had one more jump, and then it was time to get back to Mr Bhalla's for dinner. The sun was going down now, and night was falling on the jungle.

Mr Bhalla had prepared a magnificent meal of coconut rice, and there was more of the pink sherbet drink which they had all enjoyed so much earlier on. Then, because they were all tired from the journey, they decided it was time to go to bed.

As he prepared to go off to his room, Billy took Mr Bhalla aside.

'Are there many wild animals here?' he asked.

Mr Bhalla smiled. 'You don't have to be worried, Billy,' he said reassuringly. 'You're perfectly safe up in the trees. The most we get up here is the odd monkey now and then.'

'But what about in the jungle?' Billy pressed. 'Are there any . . . any tigers?'

Mr Bhalla shook his head. 'No tigers, I'm afraid. There used to be, many years ago, but they moved on. So don't worry about that.'

Billy thought for a moment.

'If there were tigers a long time ago,' he said quietly, 'does anybody in the village have a tiger skin?'

Mr Bhalla looked at Billy in surprise. 'What a strange question! But as a matter of fact, they do. We have three or four altogether. I have a very old one which my grandfather gave to me before he died. And there are a few others. But why do you ask?'

'I've had an idea,' said Billy. 'I've had an idea about how to help you. I'm not sure whether it will work, but there's no harm in trying.'

Mr Bhalla looked at Billy, and for a

moment it seemed as if his eyes would fill
with tears.

'If it might save our trees,' he said, 'then
anything – *anything* – is worth trying.'

CHAPTER 6

Billy's Plan: Part One

The next day, over a tasty breakfast of poppadoms and marmalade, Billy told everybody about his plan.

'Our only hope,' he said, 'is to scare those men away. If they become too frightened to work in the jungle, then they'll leave –'

'And the trees will be saved,' interrupted Nicola.

'Exactly,' said Billy.

There was a silence while everybody thought about this. There was no doubt it was true; but there was something which still needed to be explained.

It was Mr Gopal who asked the question which everybody was pondering.

'But how do we frighten them away?' he asked. 'It's easy to say that you will frighten somebody, but how do you do it? Those men sound pretty fierce from what Mr Bhalla has told us.'

Billy smiled. 'They may be fierce, but there's something much fiercer than they are.'

'I don't understand,' said Mr Gopal, shaking his head.

'Nor do I,' said his aunt. 'I don't see how we could frighten people like that.'

'We might not be able to frighten them,' said Billy. 'But what about *tigers?* Wouldn't they frighten them away?'

Mr Gopal snorted. 'Of course they would,'

he said. 'But where are the tigers going to come from?'

Billy smiled. This was the funny part of the plan.

'You'll see,' he said. 'But first, we have to go off and have a word with these men. Just you and I will go, Mr Gopal. The others must stay behind and get ready for tonight.'

Once Billy had explained the rest of the plan, Mr Gopal was full of enthusiasm.

'What a brilliant idea!' he cried. 'Oh, Billy, well done! I certainly wouldn't like to be in those men's shoes this evening!'

Together they climbed down the ladder from Mr Bhalla's house, while the others waved farewell from above. Then, following the well-worn path that led to the bubblegum trees, they set off purposefully on their errand.

As they got closer to the trees, they heard a sound which made their blood run cold. It was the sound of an axe chopping away at wood.

'Listen to that,' said Billy angrily. 'That's a tree being cut down.'

'I know,' said Mr Gopal. 'What a terrible waste of a bubblegum tree. A hundred years being thrown away – just like that.'

They followed the sound and in a few minutes, as they rounded a bend in the path, they heard a voice shout out ahead of them.

'Timber!' it yelled. 'Down it comes!'

Billy and Mr Gopal stopped short. A giant tree was coming down – but where would it land? Suddenly, there was a great crashing sound, and the sky above them seemed for a moment to be blotted out by a canopy of leaves and branches.

'Mr Gopal!' shouted Billy. 'Run!'

Mr Gopal was confused, but Billy grabbed him by the shirtsleeve and tugged him off the path. He was just in time, for had he not done so, Mr Gopal would have been crushed by the great tree as it fell.

'Thank you,' said Mr Gopal, wiping his

brow. 'That was a very close shave. If you hadn't pulled me away like that . . .'

He did not finish the sentence. Angry voices could now be heard, and within a few moments the two of them found themselves surrounded by men with axes in their hands and red handkerchiefs tied round their foreheads.

'What are you doing here?' snapped the tallest of the men. 'You could have got yourself killed then! You should keep away from logging, you know!'

'I'm very sorry,' said Mr Gopal. 'But my young friend here and I are on a very important mission. We certainly didn't want to disturb you.'

The polite tone of Mr Gopal's words seemed to make the man a bit calmer, and when he next spoke he sounded less angry.

'Well, just watch out in future,' he said. 'What do you want, anyway?'

Mr Gopal glanced at Billy, who now stepped forward to speak.

'Mr Gopal here is a famous photographer,' he said. 'And we have come from a very long way away to photograph some animals which we have been told are to be found in this part of the jungle. That is why we are here.'

The man looked at Billy and sneered. 'Well, you're wasting your time,' he said. 'There's nothing of any interest in this jungle.'

'Except for tigers,' said Billy quickly.

'What did you say?' said the man sharply.

'Tigers,' said Billy. 'Big tigers. They're very fierce, these ones, we believe – and very rare.'

This was the signal for all the men to burst out laughing.

'What nonsense,' said one of them. 'There are no tigers here! There aren't any tigers for miles. We should know.'

'But you must be wrong,' said Billy. 'We've been told that they're here, and in fact we've already seen one, haven't we, Mr Gopal?'

Mr Gopal nodded energetically. 'Yes. We saw a terribly big one only this morning. It was drinking from the river and I got a very good shot of it with my camera. I wish I could show you the picture, but it's not been developed yet.'

The men stopped laughing. Billy noticed that one or two of them exchanged rather nervous glances.

'And what else have you heard about these tigers?' said their leader, mockingly. 'Have you heard that they ride bicycles and eat bananas?'

Billy smiled. 'No,' he said. 'Nobody has said anything about that. But we have been told that they're man-eaters.'

As he spoke everybody became quite silent. The leader of the loggers stared at Billy, and Billy could see that there were tiny little drops of sweat forming on his forehead, just below his red handkerchief.

'Did you say man-eaters?'

'Yes,' said Billy. 'We heard that they ate

ten men further down the river. It was terrible. Only their hats were left.'

The loggers looked at one another again, and Billy decided it was time to go.

'Well,' he said. 'We mustn't keep you from

your work. You've still got lots of those trees to cut down.'

'Yes, indeed,' said Mr Gopal as they turned to leave. 'We shall just be on our way. And if you see these tigers, could you possibly let us know? I can't wait to photograph them again!'

Billy and Mr Gopal walked back down the path, leaving the men standing around the felled tree.

'It worked,' whispered Billy to Mr Gopal. 'It worked perfectly!'

Mr Gopal tried hard, but he could not help laughing.

'Oh, their faces!' he said. 'Did you see how they looked at one another for support? Those men are scared absolutely stiff!'

'Yes,' said Billy. 'Now on to part two of the plan!'

CHAPTER 7

Billy's Plan: Part Two

Back at Mr Bhalla's tree house, Billy recounted what had happened.

'It worked perfectly,' he said. 'But now we must get ready for the next stage of the plan. Mr Bhalla, have you got them?'

Mr Bhalla nodded. 'I've laid them all out in the room next door,' he said. 'And Aunt Gopal has been busy doing some stitching.'

'Good,' said Billy. 'That will be one for me, one for you, one for Mr Gopal, and one for Nicola.'

Mr Bhalla opened the door with a flourish, and there in the next room, laid out on the floor before them, were four large tiger skins. Some of them had been used as rugs, and had holes here and there, but Mr Gopal's aunt had done her best with needle and thread and these holes now looked far better.

Billy was delighted. 'I'll try mine first,' he said. 'Then you can all see what it looks like.'

He dropped to his hands and knees, and Mr Gopal draped the skin over him, tying it underneath with strings which his aunt had cunningly sewn on. It was a perfect fit.

'Oh my goodness!' exclaimed Mr Gopal. 'A tiger! A tiger in this very room!'

Billy moved about a little, and gave a roar, just for effect.

'Oh!' shouted Mr Gopal. 'My goodness me! Please help us, please! A tiger!'

Nicola tried her skin next, and she, too, looked very realistic. Then it was the turn of Mr Gopal and Mr Bhalla, both of whom made very fine tigers indeed.

'This is wonderful,' said Billy, from within his tiger skin. 'Now let's take them off and get ready to go!' They waited until it was late afternoon. India can get very hot, and nobody fancied spending much time in those heavy skins until it became a bit cooler. It was also better to wait, Billy thought, until it was getting just a little bit dark. Tigers look more frightening then.

After enjoying a final glass of pink sherbet drink on the veranda, they bundled the tiger skins into one large bundle and Mr Bhalla lowered it to the ground on a rope. Then they all climbed down the ladders to the ground and set off along the path to the jungle. Mr Gopal's aunt had been invited to go with them, but, her work on the tiger skins over, she had chosen to stay with her new friends in the village.

'We must be very quiet,' said Mr Bhalla. 'Those men have sharp hearing.'

They walked on, each person carrying a tiger skin under his arm. Each had his own thoughts. Billy thought, *I do hope this works. But what if they see the strings? What will they do to us?*

Mr Bhalla, for his part, thought, *If this fails, then they'll probably cut down the bubblegum trees even more quickly – just out of spite.*

Mr Gopal thought, *My goodness! Should I really be prowling around the jungles of India dressed in a tiger skin – at my age? Should I?*

And Nicola was just about to think, *Will the tail of my tiger skin* ... when she stopped, and every thought left her mind. For there, directly in front of her on the path, was a large snake, coiled up and hissing, poised to strike!

Nicola stood stock-still. She opened her mouth to shout out, but no sound came.

She was utterly paralysed with fright.

'Nicola,' called out Billy. 'Don't hold us up! Come on!'

'Help!' squeaked Nicola at last, just managing to sound the word. 'A snake!'

The other three stopped, and looked behind them.

'Oh no,' muttered Mr Gopal. 'A cobra! Oh, goodness!'

When Mr Bhalla saw what was happening, he stopped where he was, a short distance behind Nicola.

'Don't move,' he whispered. 'Stay absolutely still. If you move a muscle, that snake will strike. Understand?'

Nicola gave a groan. The snake was hardly more than a pace away from her, and it was clearly very angry indeed. It was her worst nightmare — her very worst nightmare — come true.

What took place next happened so quickly that Billy hardly saw what was going on. He noticed Mr Bhalla reach into his pocket and

get something out, and then, with a flick of his wrist, toss it over Nicola's shoulder. That's madness, Billy thought. The snake will strike.

The snake did strike. With a sudden lightning movement it struck, but not at Nicola. The snake struck at the small square of bubblegum which Mr Bhalla had tossed towards it. And of course, with its snake's sharp eyesight, it caught the bubblegum effortlessly. Its jaws snapped shut, the fangs sinking into the soft pink gum.

Of course the snake was now quite helpless!

'Hssss,' it went, from between its stuck-together jaws. 'Hsssss.'

'It's completely harmless now,' said Mr Bhalla, with a laugh. 'You can even step right over it if you wish, Nicola. It will take hours, maybe even days, before it gets that gum out of its mouth!'

They left the angry, but now harmless cobra behind them and continued on the path. They could see the bubblegum trees in the distance now and soon it would be time to get into the skins. Then the real excitement would start.

In the logging camp, the men had just finished work. They had had a hard day of cutting down bubblegum trees, and they were resting, while their cook prepared their evening meal. This was the time of the day that they always liked – when work was finished and they could sit about and chat outside their tents. But today there was something wrong.

'Do you think that business about tigers was true?' said one of the men. 'I thought it was quite safe round here.'

The other scratched his head. 'I don't know. Why would that man lie to us? He seemed pretty sure that he had seen something. I think there might be tigers after all.'

'If I see a tiger round here, I'm packing up

and going,' said another man. 'I don't fancy being a tiger's breakfast.'

'Neither do I,' agreed another. 'My wife doesn't want me to be eaten. She told me so herself.'

The head man got to his feet. 'Stop all this talk about tigers! I've told you before and I'll tell you again. This jungle is perfectly safe. There are no tigers.'

Just then, from some thick growth behind one of the tents, there came a noise. It was not a loud noise, but it made every head in the camp turn and stare.

'What was that?' asked one man. 'Did you hear it? There's something in those bushes over there.'

'I heard something!' shouted another, rising to his feet and huddling up with one of his friends. 'Do you think it could be . . . a . . . a . . . tiger?'

'Nonsense!' snapped the head man. 'How many times do I have to tell you? THERE ARE NO TIGERS!'

He had barely finished speaking when another noise came from the bushes. This time it was unmistakable. It was a growl!

CHAPTER 8

Tiger! Tiger!

From within the bushes, covered in his heavy tiger skin, Billy could just make out what was happening in the camp.

'They're getting nervous,' he whispered to Mr Bhalla. 'I think they heard your growl.'

'Good,' said Mr Bhalla. 'Let's just wait a few minutes. Let them think about it for a while.'

The men did think about it, and were clearly becoming more and more frightened. Several of them went to stand by the cooking fire, knowing that tigers were meant to be afraid of fire. Others stood close to the mouth of their tent, ready to dash inside if any tigers should appear.

'I think the time has come,' said Billy quietly. 'I'll go first.'

On all fours, looking quite like a fierce tiger, Billy started to move slowly out of the bushes. As he did so, he turned his tiger head from side to side, as if he were sniffing at the evening air. Then, for good measure, he growled.

When the men in the camp saw him, a great shouting broke out.

'Look!' cried one. 'Tiger! Tiger!'

'Where? Where?' shouted another.

'Over there, by the bushes! A tiger!'

As the shouting broke out, Billy darted to another clump of bushes and disappeared.

'Calm down!' shouted the head man, who

had been looking away when Billy appeared. 'You're imagining things. I tell you again, THERE ARE NO TIGERS!'

'But there was one right there,' howled one of the men. 'A great big one!'

As they argued amongst themselves, Mr Gopal crawled out of the bushes and stretched out one of his great tiger claws.

'Oh!' shouted one of the men. 'Another one! Oh, save us! Save us!'

'Where?' shouted the head man. 'Where is it?'

He turned round, and saw Mr Gopal crawling across the ground to join Billy, closely followed by Mr Bhalla and Nicola.

'Hundreds of them!' shouted one of the men. 'We're surrounded by tigers!'

This was the signal for all the men to start running around at once. Stumbling over one another, they rushed about, picking up their possessions. Then, their belongings in their arms, their axes and saws left behind on the ground, the men ran as fast as they could

down to the river, where their boat was moored.

'Grrr!' roared Mr Bhalla. 'Grrr! Grrr!'

The sound of the roaring made the men run even faster. And when they reached the river edge, they did not even climb into the boat, but leapt, like frightened rats.

In the bushes, the four tigers sat down and laughed more heartily than they had ever laughed before. Mr Gopal laughed so much that he almost choked, and he had to take his tiger head off to wipe the tears of mirth away from his eyes.

'I've never seen anybody look so frightened,' he said. 'They were terrified!'

'They won't be coming back here,' said Mr Bhalla, with a broad smile on his face. 'That's the last we'll see of them.'

'And your bubblegum trees are saved,' said Billy. 'That's the important thing.'

They could have gone home right then, but Mr Bhalla thought that it would be a good idea to stay a little longer, just in case the men looked back from the river. So they all refastened their tiger skins and got down on their hands and knees again. Then they walked out of the bushes, with the proud walk of a group of tigers who had just done a very good job.

They prowled around the abandoned camp, sniffing at the axes and giving the occasional roar. It was all going very well. It had been a wonderful plan, and nothing had gone wrong. Or at least, nothing had gone wrong until then. Then it happened.

'That was a good growl you made,' said Mr Bhalla to Billy. 'It sounded very fierce.'

'But I *didn't* growl,' said Billy. 'Maybe it was Nicola.'

'It wasn't me,' muttered Nicola from within her tiger skin.

'Nor me,' said Mr Gopal. 'I didn't growl.'

They all stopped. Who had growled? Had Mr Bhalla imagined it?

He had not. For now there came another growl, and this time it was even louder. Billy spun round, and looked behind him. There, on the edge of the camp, was a great tiger, sniffing at the air with its fine, proud tiger's nose. And this tiger, for a change, was *real*!

'Let's go!' cried Mr Bhalla. 'If we scamper away he'll think we were just a passing band of tigers. Perhaps he'll pay no attention.'

They started to run on all fours, as fast as they could. It was hard work, but they were managing quite well until Mr Gopal stumbled.

When the real tiger saw one of the other tigers fall, he pounced. He did not like the sight of these four rather peculiar-looking tigers, and he thought that he would teach this one a lesson.

The other three stopped and watched in horror as the great tiger landed on Mr Gopal's back and dug its claws into his tiger skin. Mr Gopal collapsed under the weight of the real tiger and closed his eyes. At any moment his tiger skin would come off, he thought, and the real tiger would find a tasty snack inside. What would it be like to be eaten by a tiger? Would it hurt, or would it all be over very quickly? *What will I taste like?* he thought miserably.

'Fight back, Mr Gopal!' shouted Billy. 'Remember you're a Gopal!'

Inside the tiger skin, Mr Gopal heard Billy's voice and the words stirred him. Remember you're a Gopal! Yes! He was a Gopal! He was the grandson of Sikrit Pal Praviwallah Gopal, after all, the man who had fought off a tiger by biting its tail!

Yes! That was it! Without wasting any more time, Mr Gopal reached out and grabbed the angry tiger by its tail. Then, opening his mouth as wide as he could, he popped the end of the tail inside and bit.

It did not taste very pleasant, and there was a great deal of fur, but Mr Gopal's teeth sank well into the tiger's tail and it gave a roar of pain.

'Take that!' muttered Mr Gopal from between his clamped teeth. 'That'll teach you to jump on a Gopal!'

The bite was too much for the tiger. Releasing Mr Gopal from his grip, he turned round to lick gingerly at his sore

tail. This gave Billy his chance. Rushing
forward, he helped Mr Gopal to his feet and
bundled him off down the path, followed by
the other two, all running as fast as they
possibly could. Everybody had abandoned
their tiger outfits by now, and had turned
into people again – very frightened people
running down a path with a tiger not too far
behind them.

'Will he follow us?' gasped Nicola. 'I'm
sure he'll be twice as angry now!'

'I'm afraid he might,' panted Mr Bhalla.

'Tigers get very cross about this sort of thing. They're not ones to give up easily. We shall have to climb a tree.'

On hearing Mr Bhalla's suggestion, they all stopped and looked about them. The path on either side of them was flanked by great towering trees, and if they managed to scale one of these then the tiger might walk right past them.

'What about this one?' said Billy, pointing to a particularly tall tree. 'There are enough low branches to give us a start.'

'A splendid idea,' said Mr Bhalla. 'You children go first and Mr Gopal and I will follow.'

It was not a difficult tree to climb, and soon all four of them were perched right up at the top, looking down through the leaves to the path far below. Now all they had to do was wait until the tiger went past. It would soon realise it had lost them, and all they would have to do then would be to wait a little while before they climbed down and made their way home.

The minutes went past slowly and Billy was beginning to wonder whether the tiger had gone in the other direction. Then suddenly Mr Bhalla touched Billy on the arm and pointed downwards.

'Tiger,' he whispered. 'Right below us.'

Billy looked down. There on the path below them was the beautiful, sinewy figure of the tiger, padding slowly along, its nose raised to sniff the breeze for the scent of its enemies.

'Oh dear,' said Mr Gopal. 'It looks very cross.'

'Well, it's not going to find us,' said Billy quietly. 'So you don't have to –'

He was about to say 'worry', but before he had time to do so a terrible thing happened. Mr Gopal had taken a handkerchief out of his pocket to mop his brow and had unfortunately dropped it. Down through the leaves drifted the large white square of cloth, right down to the path, to land exactly in front of the angry tiger.

Of course the tiger looked up in surprise and saw, directly above it, four frightened human beings sitting on a very high branch. At the sight of this, it let out a great roar, which seemed to fill the forest with sound before it died away.

'Oh my goodness!' wailed Mr Gopal. 'We are going to be entirely eaten up. This terrible beast will shin up our tree and eat us up – one, two, three, four. Every one of us.'

But Mr Gopal was wrong. The tiger looked at the trunk of the tree, stretched its claws in and out, and then yawned.

'He's too lazy,' said Mr Bhalla. 'That's a typical tiger for you! He knows that he doesn't even have to try to climb the tree. All he has to do is lie there until we come down.'

The tiger looked up again, gave another growl, and then lay down at the foot of the tree. There was no need for him to waste his energy – his lunch was up the tree, hanging on to a branch, but sooner or later it would have to come down, and by then he hoped he would have an even sharper appetite!

CHAPTER 9

Bubblegum to the Rescue

They sat on their high branches, looking
down at the patient tiger and wondering how
long it would be before one of them was
overcome by sleep and fell off. It could be a
day or two, if they were lucky, or it could be
before that. Whenever it would be, it was not
a nice thought. Then, after about an hour, Mr
Bhalla suddenly let out a cry.

'I've had a wonderful idea,' he said. 'Why didn't I think of it before?'

'What is it?' asked Mr Gopal. 'Could it possibly help us?'

'Yes,' said Mr Bhalla. 'Do you know what sort of tree this is?'

'A bubblegum tree,' said Billy. 'Or at least it looks like one.'

'Precisely,' said Mr Bhalla. 'And it's a very nice juicy one at that. If I cut a little hole here, sap will come out by the bucketful.'

'But what use would that be?' asked Nicola. 'It won't do us any good to sit up here and chew bubblegum!'

Mr Bhalla laughed. 'Indeed it would not,' he agreed. 'What I propose is that we make a gumgee rope out of the gum and then one of us can bounce down, give that tiger a bit of a fright, and then bounce back!'

Everybody was silent. It was a most peculiar plan, but then the Bubblegummies were most peculiar people.

Then Billy broke the silence.

'But who will jump?' he asked.

Mr Bhalla smiled. 'I was thinking you might like to do it, Billy,' he said, with a smile. 'I hear that you were gumgee jumping last night in the village, and you did it very well.'

Billy swallowed hard. He really had no choice. They had to do something about the tiger and he might as well be the one to do it. But a gumgee jump on to a tiger's back? That sounded even worse than biting a tiger's tail!

Mr Bhalla made a hole in the bark of the bubblegum tree and had soon extracted a large lump of soft pink sap in his cupped hands. He passed this to Nicola, showing her how to twist it into a rope. Then he made another hole and collected more sap and passed that on to Billy. Soon everybody had twisted a long piece of gummy rope, which Mr Bhalla tied together to make one long gumgee jumping rope.

'Now,' he said, tying one end of the rope to

their branch. 'Let's attach the other end round you, Billy, and then you'll be ready.'

'But what do I do once I get down there?' asked Billy, his voice unsteady with fear.

'Pull its whiskers,' said Mr Bhalla. 'That's one thing which a tiger can't stand. If you pull its whiskers it will go away soon enough.'

Billy looked down through the leaves to the waiting tiger. He closed his eyes and counted. One, two, three . . . Now! Taking a deep breath, he cast himself off the branch, shooting down through the leaves, straight towards the tiger. Then, with a sudden lurch, he felt the bubblegum rope tighten and slow down his fall.

Mr Bhalla had calculated the length of the rope to perfection. Billy found himself just above the rather astonished tiger, and he was able to reach out and give the tiger's whiskers a good tweak. The tiger roared out in fury and slashed at Billy with his great claws, but he was too late – the bubblegum rope had yanked Billy up again and the next thing the tiger saw was the boy disappearing through the leaves!

Down went Billy for the second time, and again he was able to give the tiger's whiskers a good pull before he shot up again into the leaves. The tiger was even more furious this time, and by the time it had happened for a third time, the animal's patience was exhausted. With a great roar of disgust, it turned on its tail and shot off down the path, to vanish in the undergrowth.

'He's had enough,' shouted Mr Bhalla triumphantly. 'I knew he wouldn't like that! I knew it!'

They waited a few minutes to make sure that the tiger did not come back. Then, once they were sure it was safe to do so, they climbed back down the tree and began the journey back to the village.

'I feel rather sorry for that poor tiger,' said Billy to Mr Bhalla as they walked home. 'I'm sure we made him feel rather miserable.'

'Yes,' said Mr Bhalla. 'But you must remember that we also did him a big favour. By saving the forest, we've preserved a home for him. If the loggers had cut down all the trees, he would have had nowhere to go.'

'So even if he is rather cross with us, we've still saved his life,' said Billy.

'Exactly,' said Mr Bhalla. 'Just so.'

When everybody in the village heard about what had happened, they were overjoyed.

'Our trees are saved!' they cried. 'And we owe it all to your plan, Billy.'

Billy, of course, was very modest. 'I was only one of the tigers,' he said. 'Everybody was brave.'

They were too tired to celebrate that night, and decided that they would have a village party the next day. So they all went to bed in their rooms high up in Mr Bhalla's tree house, and they all, in their different ways, dreamed about what had happened that day. In Billy's dream he was prowling around in a tiger skin, growling through his teeth. In Nicola's dream there was a snake blowing bubbles through its tightly-clamped jaws. Mr Bhalla dreamed of bubblegum trees, safe again. And Mr Gopal – well, he dreamed that he was biting a tiger's tail while his grandfather, Sikrit Pal Praviwallah Gopal, looked on with pride.

The next morning, the entire village was up early, getting ready for the party. Great dishes of food were prepared in the high tree-kitchens, sending delicious odours wafting through the branches. The school was closed for the day – to mark the occasion – and everybody was in a festive mood.

Mr Bhalla was particularly excited. He dressed in his finest outfit – a gold and white tunic which had belonged to his father, who had been an official elephant driver, a *mahout*, to the Maharajah of Chandipore. Billy, who had not brought any special clothes with him, was lent a party tunic by one of the Bubblegummie boys, and Nicola was given a green and gold sari to wear. Everybody looked very smart indeed.

The party began with a feast. This was a magnificent affair, with all sorts of delicious foods set out on broad green leaves freshly picked from banana trees. There were curries and pickles and large dishes of dried coconut. There were poppadoms stacked one hundred high, and great mounds of bananas fried in sugared yoghurt!

But most delicious of all was a dish which had been made by Mr Gopal's aunt. She had not wasted her time while the others were away being chased by a tiger. She had been learning recipes from her new friends and, with a little help, she had now cooked the most wonderful bubblegum pudding anybody had ever tasted. It was an extraordinary dish – a pudding you could chew on for as long as you liked and then blow into great big bubbles before you swallowed. The Bubblegummie children were used to this

sort of thing, of course, but for Billy and Nicola it was quite unlike anything they had ever eaten before, and twice as nice.

After the feast there were competitions, including a most exciting game of tree hide-and-seek. This was far more thrilling – and dangerous – than an ordinary game of hide-and-seek, as you had to hide in the branches, which was not always easy. There was also a gumgee-jumping competition – which Nicola won – and, finally, a bubblegum-blowing contest. Billy entered this, and did quite well, but not as well as Mr Gopal himself, who blew a bubble so large that even the Bubblegummies were impressed.

'We are so very grateful to you,' said Mr Bhalla, as the party came to an end. 'It would have been a tragedy if those men had destroyed our bubblegum trees. Now, thanks to you, the trees will survive. And of course we shall be able to send Mr Gopal his supplies again.'

'It was no trouble at all,' said Billy. 'I'm glad to have helped.'

He knew, of course, that it could all have turned out quite differently. The snake could have bitten Nicola. The men could have guessed that the tigers weren't real. The real tiger could have eaten Mr Gopal. But none of these things had happened, and so there was no point in worrying about it.

They left the following morning. Mr Bhalla helped them into the flying boat, and then he and just about everybody from the village stood at the edge of the river and waved as the ancient plane taxied out to start its take-off.

'Goodbye!' shouted Mr Bhalla, as the plane began to skim over the water. 'Come back and see us soon!'

'We shall!' cried Billy, waving from his window.

Then the plane was in the air, and the river and the jungle fell away beneath them.

They had a long flight ahead of them, but Mr Bhalla had given them plenty of bubblegum for the trip. So that would keep them busy enough.

As the plane gained height, Billy craned his neck to get a last glimpse of the ground below them. There was the village, with its walkways and swinging bridges; there was Mr Bhalla's house in its tall tree. And there, of course, were the bubblegum trees themselves, towering higher than all the other trees, and safe now – Billy hoped – for at least another hundred years.